W9-BHL-669

HORSE RAID
The Making of a Warrior

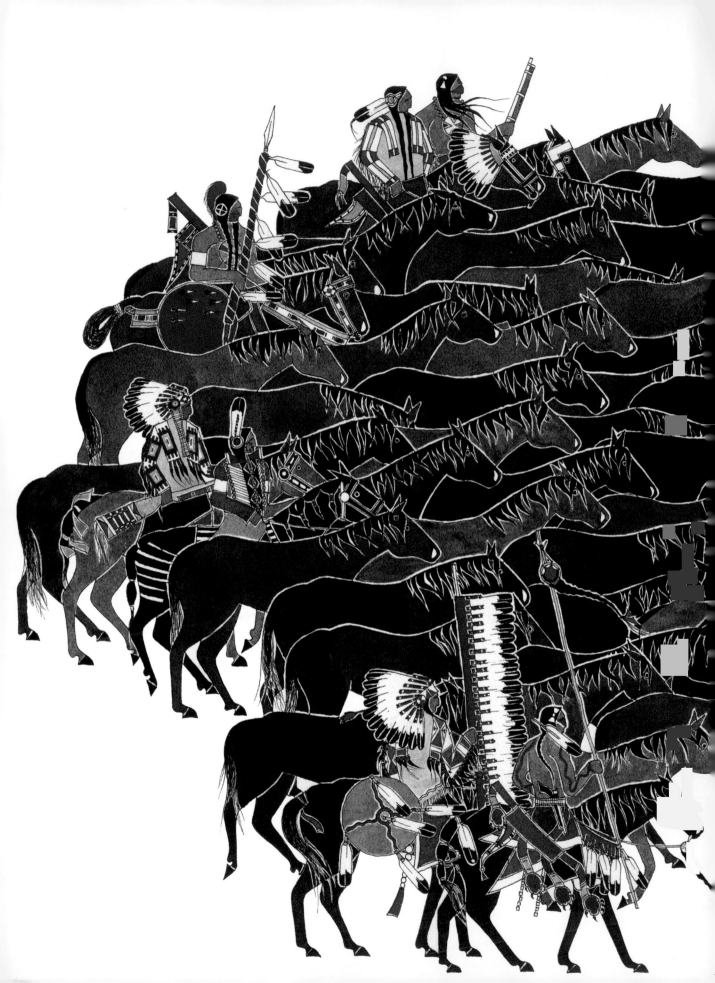

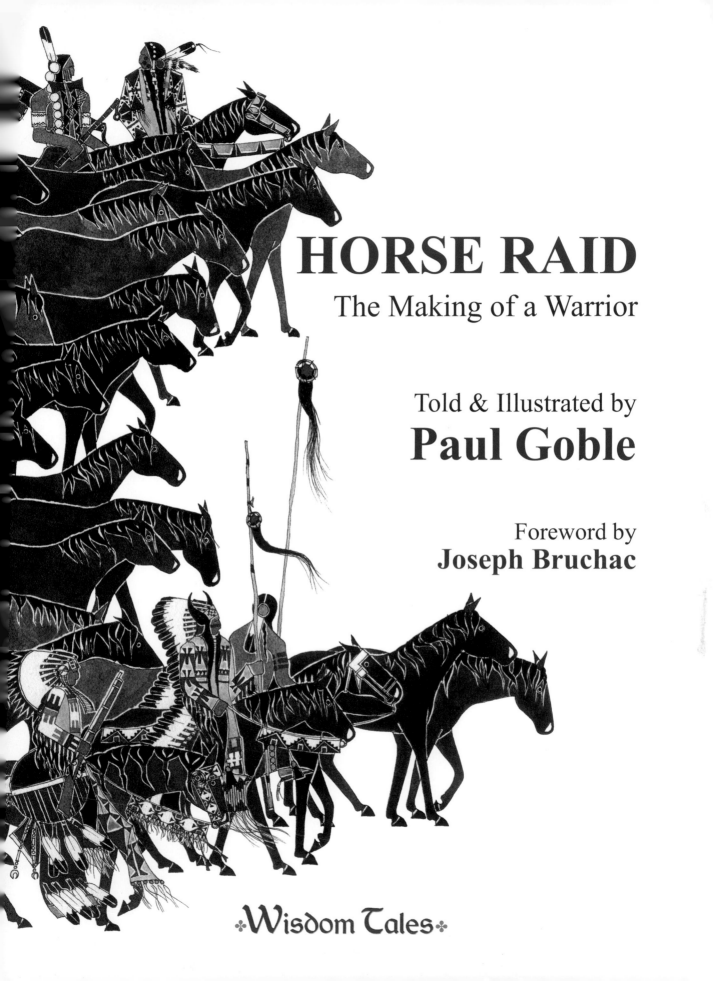

HORSE RAID
The Making of a Warrior

Told & Illustrated by
Paul Goble

Foreword by
Joseph Bruchac

✤Wisdom Tales✤

Horse Raid: The Making of a Warrior
© Paul Goble, 2014

Wisdom Tales is an imprint of World Wisdom, Inc.

Wisdom Tales wishes to thank the South Dakota Art
Museum for their assistance in the loan and scanning
of the original artwork of this title.

Horse Raid is a revised and updated edition of Lone
Bull's Horse Raid, © Paul and Dorothy Goble, 1973,
published by Bradbury Press, New York.

Cover: Original painting by Paul Goble

All rights reserved. No part of this book may be used
or reproduced in any manner without written permis-
sion, except in critical articles and reviews.

Printed in China on acid-free paper
Production Date: January 2014; Plant & Location: Printed
by Everbest Printing (Guangzhou, China), Co. Ltd
Job / Batch # 118441

Library of Congress Cataloging-in-Publication Data

Goble, Paul, author, illustrator.
[Lone Bull's horse raid]
Horse raid : the making of a warrior / told & illustrated
by Paul Goble ; foreword by Joseph Bruchac.
pages cm
Originally published by Macmillan in 1973 under title:
Lone Bull's horse raid.
Summary: Two young Sioux join in a raiding party to
capture horses from some neighboring Crows.
Includes bibliographical references.
ISBN 978-1-937786-25-0 (hardcover : alk. paper) [1.
Indians of North America--Fiction.] I. Title.
PZ7.G5384Ho 2014, [Fic]--dc23 2013050110

For information address Wisdom Tales,
P.O. Box 2682, Bloomington, Indiana 47402-2682

www.wisdomtalespress.com

CENTRAL ARKANSAS LIBRARY SYSTEM
CHILDREN'S LIBRARY
LITTLE ROCK, ARKANSAS

*for **Lakota Ishnala***

Foreword

Few non-Indians have immersed themselves as deeply in the histories and traditions of the Native nations of the Great Plains as Paul Goble. Through his distinguished career as an artist and a storyteller, he's always paid close attention to the details that often elude those who try to write about or illustrate Native American stories but lack his knowledge and desire for veracity.

That's one reason why this new edition of *Lone Bull's Horse Raid*, first published in 1973, is so welcome.

Another reason is his writing. It is as direct, informative, and clear as a Lakota elder recounting the tale to his grandchildren. The story moves at a pace as rapid and exciting as the horse raid it describes. Here's a passage about getting ready outside the enemy camp:

> I took off my leggings to walk more quietly. Charging Bear cut cottonwood bark and we rubbed the cool sap over our bodies because horses like the sweet smell and would not fear strangers in the dark.

Then there are the illustrations. Goble's style has always been distinctly his own, including his use of a white "spirit line" around his figures. But it also draws upon and honors the ancient Plains traditions of stylized art that we see on parfleche bags and the tanned buffalo skin "winter counts" where a year's important events were pictured.

One should note that American Indian traditions of raiding other tribes for horses were viewed as an honorable pursuit by all the native nations of the Great Plains. It was not "stealing" in the European sense, but something done to earn honor amongst one's people as much as it was to obtain those horses. In fact, it was common for men who were successful in taking horses from another tribe to then give away many of those same horses to one's own tribal members who needed them.

It's also interesting to note that the way of life Goble presents so brilliantly only began after Spanish herds escaped and spread across the center of the continent following the great Pueblo Revolt of 1680. The time of

mounted Indians hunting buffalo and raiding for horses lasted less than two centuries and ended abruptly during the last third of the 19th century with the brutal near-extermination of the American bison by white hunters.

This book tells a story of that time as well as anyone has ever told it. Within these pages you'll experience the bravery, tension, and triumph of a young man on his first raid. It's a trip worth taking.

Joseph Bruchac

Author's Note

Horse raiding continued for several years after the people were hemmed in on reservations because this was the traditional way for a young man to gain a good reputation in the tribe. But the raiders were finally stopped by the White Man's law, which, instead of recognition and praise, gave a jail sentence as the only reward.

Until quite recently there were old men living on the reservations who had taken part in raids when they were young. While they were in general reluctant to speak to white men about their part in battles with the U.S. Army, for fear of punishment, they were proud to talk about their experiences in fights with other tribes. George Bird Grinnell, James Willard Schultz, and others, who had lived with Indian people during the buffalo days, recorded accounts of war-parties and horse raiding.

These accounts are exciting and valuable for the insight they give into Plains Indian warfare. The accounts vary greatly in their details, but the features which are common to them all have been woven into this description of a successful horse raid. Lone Bull is a fourteen year old Oglala Sioux boy; he is a typical boy from any Plains Indian tribe about 150 years ago. The "enemy" is the Crow tribe because at that time these two peoples considered that capturing each others' horses was a point of honor.

About Horse Raiding

The battles between the Plains Indians and the United States Cavalry have been fought so many times in novels and on the screen that today it is almost forgotten that the tribes also fought among themselves. Sitting Bull, the Sioux leader at General Custer's defeat on the Little Bighorn, is always pictured as fighting the soldiers. In reality only twenty-one of his sixty-three war honors, or "coups," were won fighting the white men; the rest were won in battles with enemy tribes.

Raiding each others' horse herds was the greatest single cause of inter-tribal wars; it gave great excitement and offered rich rewards. Horses were the only valuable property, and apart from the occasional female captive, no other plunder was sought. To steal horses from an enemy tribe was honorable, whereas stealing in the usual sense was dishonest and intolerable for a closely-knit nomadic society.

The Indians needed horses for chasing buffalo and carrying their tipis and belongings. A man with more horses than he needed was in a position to trade or lend them in return for payment or other favors. Wealth was therefore largely measured by the size of a man's herd and there are records of men who owned four or five hundred horses. These men were regarded with a mixture of admiration and contempt for hoarding. The men most admired were those repeatedly successful in capturing horses and who afterwards gave them all away to their friends; this showed they were confident of capturing more in the future, and next to bravery, generosity was the virtue most admired. As an old man, Chief White Bull of the Sioux was proud to boast of the 142 horses he had given away during his lifetime.

Children grew up in a society which held the warrior as its highest ideal, and at every step in life were encouraged to follow the example of the bravest men. A father would hold up his baby son towards the rising sun and pray: "Oh sun! Make this boy strong and brave. May he die in battle rather than from old age or sickness." Stories of raiding enemy horse herds fired young boys to imitate the warriors, and they were present at gatherings where men competed in telling and re-enacting their brave deeds. As a boy grew up he saw that only men who had proved themselves warriors were looked up to and their words heeded in the tribal councils, and later he also learned that no girl would ever look favorably on him until he had proved his bravery and won the right to wear an eagle feather.

There was fierce competition among the warriors to win personal glory. Any man could shoot and kill an enemy from a distance; it demanded little courage and received no honor. To prove his bravery a warrior deliberately exposed himself to danger by first striking an enemy with a coup-stick or bow before killing him. Such heroism won many battles against the soldiers, and after his bitter experience at the Battle of the Little Bighorn, Major Marcus Reno described the Plains Indians as "the finest light cavalry in the world."

Anyone could lead a horse raiding party, but the warriors usually followed an experienced leader who had a reputation for success. As leader he was responsible for the safety of every member and if any were lost his reputation might suffer. Parties rarely numbered more than fifteen and often there were only two or three individuals involved. They left camp quietly

so that if they were unsuccessful they could return home as quietly as they had left without questions being asked. Festivities and praise were reserved for those who were successful and returned home without loss of life. Winter was the favorite season because it relieved the monotony of the long winter months. Parties left on foot or on horseback; those on foot could hide themselves and their trail more easily but were vulnerable to attack from mounted enemies. The aim of the horse raiders might be to run off some of the enemy's herds which grazed outside the camp circle, but this needed no special skill. The ideal was to creep into the enemy camp at night and take the fastest horses, the buffalo runners as they were called, which were jealously guarded and picketed outside their owners' tipis. In doing this the warrior risked losing his life and it was counted a minor war honor.

Young boys specially sought such honors because it was their first step towards recognition as brave men. They went more for the excitement and glamour than for the horses. It was their initiation into the warrior's life. On their first trip they might be expected to serve their seniors, fetching water and wood for the fire and helping in various small ways. They suffered practical jokes and teasing but were content to put up with this in return for the privilege of being members of the group. When battles were fought to regain lost horses, it was usually the boys who were in the forefront in their efforts to outdo each other. They had a reputation to make, whereas the older men had proved themselves and took fewer risks. Whether a boy distinguished himself or not on his first trip, he was from then on considered grown-up and would be invited to join one of the tribal warrior societies.

Sometimes a man went horse raiding because he had received a dream or sign of future success. A medicine man might be consulted about the interpretation of the dream and if he gave encouragement a group would soon be organized and on its way. If not, the idea was abandoned at once. Indeed at any time a member, or the whole party, might suddenly decide to return home if anyone had a foreboding of failure or death. The Indian had a unique ability to interpret both his instincts and natural surroundings. As he roamed the vastness of the prairie he read and understood every natural sign. There are many instances where a coyote's bark or the call of a crow were understood as warnings; at other times it was just a compelling presentiment of imminent danger which saved the raiders from certain death.

Wherever the Plains Indian went, whether horse raiding, moving camp, or chasing buffalo, he put his trust in his horse. In the chase or in times of danger he expected great endurance from his mount; this was no different from what he himself was prepared to endure when the occasion demanded. He did not attribute human thoughts or feelings to his horse, nor attempt to train him in behavior which was uncharacteristic or degrading. He recognized that his horse had a soul. He saw that the horse was an important part of the great mystery of the universe around him and therefore, like all things in nature, deserved his deepest respect. He saw horses in his dreams and visions; he sang of them in his songs and remembered them in his stories; he painted them on rocks and on his buffalo robe, his shield and on his tipi. And at the end, when death came, a man's favorite buffalo runner was killed at his grave so that he could ride the longest of all trails along the Milky Way to the Spirit World.

HORSE RAID
The Making of a Warrior

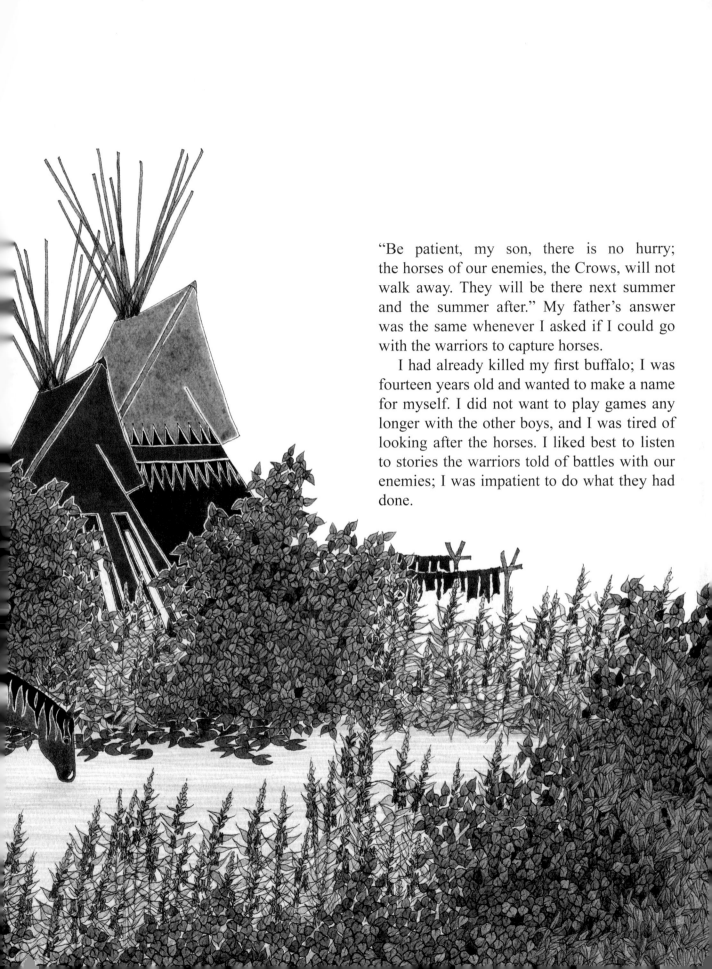

"Be patient, my son, there is no hurry; the horses of our enemies, the Crows, will not walk away. They will be there next summer and the summer after." My father's answer was the same whenever I asked if I could go with the warriors to capture horses.

I had already killed my first buffalo; I was fourteen years old and wanted to make a name for myself. I did not want to play games any longer with the other boys, and I was tired of looking after the horses. I liked best to listen to stories the warriors told of battles with our enemies; I was impatient to do what they had done.

Charging Bear thought as I did and we talked about joining the first horse raiding party which left camp. We were friends, closer than brothers, and had agreed that if one was ever in trouble the other would always help, even if it meant death. One day in the Moon of Dark Red Cherries, July, my father was choosing men to go with him after Crow horses. It was the chance we had waited for. We decided to follow their trail and to join them when we were too far from home to be sent back.

My grandfather must have guessed; he knew most of my secrets and when we were beyond hearing said: "No man can help another to be brave, grandson, but through brave deeds you may become a leader one day. Tomorrow when the sky begins to turn yellow, I shall be waiting over there among the trees by the creek with your horse and everything needed for your journey. Bring your bow. Be careful; I have heard it said that the women are watching to make sure you do not run off."

After dark the men came silently one at a time to our tipi. They did not want it known they were going after horses because many would have wanted to join them, but a large party leaves a broad trail which is difficult to hide. My father had chosen nine experienced men who knew the land of the Crows. His friend Thunder Horse was a great warrior, always restless when sitting at home. When he entered the lodge, father gave him the place of honor at the back across from the entrance.

When they were all assembled mother placed food before them. Afterwards a pipe was passed from hand to hand around the lodge, each one asking the spirits to grant success. I can still see my father as he leaned forward to draw with a stick in the dry earth. He spoke of the trail they would take, the best places to cross the rivers, and the most likely places the Crows would be camped. They all spoke in low voices until long into the night, and when the sounds in the camp grew small, the pipe was returned to the rack at the back of the fireplace. It was time to go. While the men left quietly, my father sat for a time staring into the fire and eating a little food. Afterwards he searched for his things, mother helping and telling him to be careful. I heard him saddle his favorite buffalo runner, and then he was gone.

The night seemed long waiting for the dawn. I was thinking of many things; listening to the murmur of the creek and the breeze rustling the cottonwood leaves. I lay on my back looking up through the smoke hole at the stars. How slowly they move . . .

Hehey! It was light when I opened my eyes! My mother and little sister were still sleeping. I took down the quiver from the pole above my bed, felt under the cover for a peg, cut the thong and slipped underneath. I strode past the tipis with my blanket drawn over my face so I would not be recognized, and once beyond the edge of the camp, ran off to the creek. There stood Charging Bear and my grandfather holding my horse.

"*Hau*, grandson, here you are." I was too upset to say I had slept, but he knew and said in a cheerful voice: "Your grandmother has packed everything you need in the saddlebag. Look! The sun touches the tipi poles and the women will soon be about. Go now!"

We followed the creek up into the hills and found the tracks where the men had waited for each other. The morning was bright, and looking back we saw thin wisps of smoke from the cooking fires rising in the still air. My mother would already have missed me; perhaps she had sent my uncle to search for me.

We traveled as fast as we could all day, sometimes losing the trail and then finding it again. When it was too dark to see we hobbled our horses in some grass beside a stream. I rolled up in my blanket but could not sleep. It was my first night away from home and every small sound startled me. I felt a coward, Charging Bear too. We thought we would never be brave; we saw things in the dark that were not there. We hardly slept all night.

We set off as the sky brightened, and when the sun was still low over the prairie we came to where the men had spent the night. I climbed a hill with a wide view hoping to see them, but nothing disturbed the prairie-chicken dancing among the sagebrush. We pressed on as fast as our horses could go. Our friends, too, were traveling fast; we did not see them that night nor the next. By then I thought we must be nearing Crow hunting grounds and I was afraid we might never catch up with them.

Early on the fourth day we came to where they had killed an antelope and had built a fire. The ashes were still hot and the remains of their meal scattered around. We were enjoying some pieces and wondering why they had left so much, when riders yelling war cries suddenly appeared over the edge of a gulch

not a stone's throw away. I grabbed my horse's reins, and then realized they were our friends.

"So my son follows our trail like a coyote to eat the scraps we leave!" my father said laughingly. "We have been watching you like the mountain lion waits for the little wolf. It was to make your heart strong. It is good that you have come. I am proud, my son. Come and eat." Later I told Charging Bear what a fright they had given me, and how glad I was that my father was not angry.

By now we were entering Crow hunting grounds and we traveled at night or in the early mornings. We walked our horses so they did not tire, taking care not to frighten the buffalo in case an enemy should see them running. When crossing high ground we waited while scouts in wolf skin disguises peeped over the top. During the heat of the day we hid among trees by the river and tried to rest, but the biting-flies were troublesome. We took turns to keep watch and before setting out again we took a swim.

On the seventh day we came to a broad trail where many people and horses had passed days before. We climbed a high ridge where we hid in some thick pines, while two scouts went ahead to look for the camp.

The shadows were getting long when the scouts returned, and by the time they led us to a hilltop the sun had already set. Though many years ago, I can still see the view which unfolded before my eyes: about a long bowshot from us, two Crow men were talking and enjoying the evening air. Horses, many hundreds of them, were grazing on the slopes, and away down the valley beside the creek were their tipis partly hidden among the trees and darkening shadows.

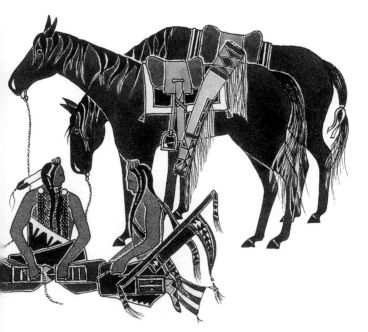

As darkness fell we watched the Crows driving their horses to the creek. I was excited; I think I was already driving home horses and could hear my grandfather singing praise-songs. We rode down the valley and tied up our horses in a cottonwood grove. Everyone made ready. I took off my leggings to walk more quietly. Charging Bear cut cottonwood bark and we rubbed the cool sap over our bodies because horses like the sweet smell and would not fear strangers in the dark. "My friends," whispered my father, "tomorrow the Crow women will weep for their lost horses and their men will give chase to dry their eyes. We are not afraid. We are Oglalas! *Koya kuye*, let's go."

We kept close to the creek where the willows were thickest. Our footsteps startled the silence and I kept close to the man ahead. A sniff of cooking smoke drifted among the trees and then the leaders stopped, for there, over the bushes, were the tops of tipis glowing faintly from the fires inside. Now we could hear women's voices and a baby crying. Suddenly a dog barked, then others joined in and it seemed that every dog in the camp was barking. Men and women shouted to quieten them and after a while there was silence again. We listened. There were footsteps in the grass ahead. Then they stopped. I think I was ready to run. Everyone held his breath—my heart was beating like a berry-masher. Then the footsteps retreated; the Crow must have been afraid to look closer in the shadows, or perhaps he thought it was just a skunk which had set the dogs barking.

We waited, listening to the crickets and cicadas. The Seven Stars were turning and I knew it was near the middle of the night; the people were sleeping, and by sunrise we had to be far away with the horses. My father whispered it was time, and that I should stay close to him; Charging Bear went with Thunder Horse, nervous of us youngsters. We closed in and were soon between the tipis. My father signaled me to stop, and I crouched by a pathway which the women had made when going to and fro carrying water. After what seemed a long time I heard the thud of hooves and my father appeared leading two horses. "Be careful," he whispered, "I saw a man go into a lodge over there."

I was alone. I felt eyes were watching me as I moved among the dark shapes of the picketed horses and lodges. It was something like the game I had played so often back home, but this was different; at any moment I expected to feel an arrow or hear a gun go off. I can never forget the fear I felt that night. The horses had cropped the grass short, the ground was flat, and there was nowhere to hide. With my eyes in all directions I approached a tall painted tipi set apart a little from the rest. There was a beautiful black horse tied before the door. His body glistened like dew-covered cobwebs in the starlight. I felt I had to have that horse, but I saw that his tether disappeared

through a dark hole under the lodge cover which was raised a little. The owner must have prized him greatly; perhaps he slept with the tether tied around his wrist. I should have tried at another lodge, but I had to have him, and I walked slowly to him, all the while keeping my eyes on the black hole at the base of the lodge. As I approached him, he suddenly strode off, shaking his mane and blowing sharply down his nose. Then he stopped abruptly at the end of his tether. Had the owner felt him pull? I knew some horses were trained to wake their owner. I kept still for what seemed a long while, trying to see under the lodge cover. There was no movement; I took hold of the tether, cut it, and pulling gently, walked towards him.

Just as I led him off a shot rang out next to my ear! Quicker than it takes to tell, the Crow had pulled up the lodge cover and was running at me with a tomahawk. Somehow I managed to jump on the frightened horse, let out a loud cry and galloped off.

The camp awoke like an overturned ant heap; men, naked except for their breach-cloths, were running from the lodge, horses were prancing at their pickets, and people were shouting to one another. At the edge of the camp I ran into Charging Bear. He jumped up behind me and I shouted to hold on as we galloped out into the open away from the tipis.

The men cracked their lariats over the crowding and rearing horse, yelling and flapping their blankets to get them moving. With only the light of the stars, it seemed like we had taken every horse in the camp. We worked hard to keep them moving, stumbling down steep slopes and into ravines, and splashing across rivers. Bushes whipped my face and scratched my body, branches tore at my hair, and the dust filled my eyes and mouth.

We drove them hard all night; many strayed or became tired out, but there was no time to wait for stragglers. When the sun's first rays touched the tops of the mountains behind us, we stopped no longer than it took to put our saddles on fresh horses. Then on again, driving them, hurrying.

From time to time my father would turn off to one side up a slight rise to see if we were being followed. The trail we left was broad and easy to follow. Thunder Horse rode ahead to pick out the best trail while we followed with riders out on both flanks to keep the horses bunched up. I rode with Charging Bear.

By the time the sun was overhead we began to hope the Crows had given up the chase, but soon we saw a cloud of dust way back on our trail. Everyone hurried to catch a fresh horse; the Crows would soon be upon us. There were no trees anywhere to give us cover; the ground was cut by gullies leading into a dry creek with steep sides. We drove the horses down into the bottom.

"My friends," said my father, "this is a good place to hide; we will take them by surprise. I am going back with Thunder Horse to lead the Crows here. Nobody must show himself until they are right upon us. Then shoot! Fight bravely! Their horses will be tired with carrying them since daybreak." We watched my father and Thunder Horse go back a little way on our trail; they sat down, pretending to smoke.

Coming closer the leading Crow warriors stopped, pointing; taking out their weapons, they charged, whipping their horses on both sides. Our friends jumped up and as they galloped away Thunder Horse's mount was shot beneath him, and I thought he would be killed. He turned to face the Crows singing

his death song and shooting his arrows fast, determined that more than one would die before him. But my father turned; bending low over his horse's neck he circled back right in front of the oncoming Crows and took his friend up behind him. It was a brave thing to do, and I never knew how all the bullets and arrows missed them. The Crows were so excited and sure of killing them that they never noticed us hiding in the gully.

Hoka hey! Hoka hey! Charge! I was among the first to whip my horse up over the top. I have never seen men so surprised: the Crows jerked back on their reins raising clouds of dust. The next moment they were wheeling about, rearing and bumping into each other in their efforts to get away, leaving one of their friends on the ground, dead at our first shot. Another could not turn fast enough; Fire Wolf swung his tomahawk, knocking him backwards out of his saddle.

They scattered and soon we were strung out chasing them over the prairie. I gained on a Crow riding a dark bay, but in my excitement I dropped my arrow. He kept glancing back as he tried to reload an old muzzle-loading gun. He slipped a ball down the barrel and banged the butt on his saddle to ram it home, but as he turned to aim, my arrow knocked him forward. He let go his gun, clinging to his horse's mane, and fell when I struck him with my bow. He was young; maybe, like me, it was his first fight and if he had been a little quicker loading his gun he might have got me first. By the time I had caught his horse and found his gun, my friends had disappeared over the rise chasing the enemy. Thunder Horse, still afoot, had signaled Charging Bear to bring him a horse. "Hurry, we must get the horses started for home right away. These Crows have had enough, but others may still be coming."

Our friends soon caught us up, Spotted Elk with a scalp tied to the tip of his bow. Far behind us the Crows watched, sitting on their horses, waiting to pick up their dead comrades. We kept the herd moving at a steady pace because we thought they might follow, seeking an opportunity to take back their horses.

Dark thunder clouds gathered on every side as darkness fell, and my father told us we should stop during the storm.

When the prairie awoke next morning everything had been made new by the rain. Even the flowers looked brighter, and the scent of sage and thirsty earth filled the air. Every little gully was filled with new earth and pools of water lay in the hollows where the day before the buffalo had wallowed in the dust to keep off the flies. The Thunder Beings had taken pity on us and sent the rain to wash away all signs of our trail. We saw no more of the Crows. The horses were scattered in every direction, grazing where they had strayed during the storm. It was near the middle of the morning before we had rounded up the last of them.

When we were almost home we stopped to bathe, and we put on our shirts and all our best things, and painted our faces because we had been successful. Long willow sticks were cut and the three scalps tied to the ends. My father gave me one to carry saying: "Give this to a woman who mourns a relative killed by the enemy. Tell her to grieve no more, and let her hold it aloft as she leads us in the victory dance tonight."

I rode the beautiful black horse; he knew how proud I felt. He was tall and powerful, yet gentle and eager to do everything I told him. Charging Bear rode beside me on a bay. When our camp came in view over the willows at a bend in the river, we whipped up the horses to a hard gallop.

All about me the air was filled with the sweet smell of horses: blacks, whites, bays, and sorrels, proud of their beauty, prancing this way and that, their manes and tails flying like wind-driven clouds about them. Even the horses out on the prairies lifted their heads, neighing their welcome to the new horses. *Hetchetu whelo!*

How glad I was to be home! How proud as I rode beside my father to our tipi! There were tears in my mother's eyes as she greeted us. I jumped down from the black horse and put the reins in my grandfather's hands. I wanted him to have the best horse I had brought back.

There was feasting and dancing throughout the camp for many days. To show his happiness my father invited the old and the poor to a feast. Afterwards when everyone was filled with meat he gave away the horses. We both gave and gave until our hearts were strong with giving.

Now at last I stood before them as a warrior and told all that I had done.

In a sacred manner
I live,
To the heavens
I gaze;
In a sacred manner
I live,
My horses are many!

References

Stories of horse raiding and battles between the tribes will be found in these books:

Blish, Helen H. *A Pictographic History of the Oglala Sioux: The Drawings of Amos Bad Heart Bull*. Lincoln: University of Nebraska Press, 1967.

Densmore, Frances. *Teton Sioux Music*. Lincoln: University of Nebraska Press, 1992.

Ewers, John C. *The Horse in Blackfoot Indian Culture: With Comparative Material from Other Western Tribes*. Washington: Smithsonian Institution Press, 1979.

Grinnell, George B. *Pawnee Hero Stories and Folk Tales: With Notes on the Origin, Customs, and Character of the Pawnee People*. Lincoln: University of Nebraska Press, 1990.

———. *By Cheyenne Campfires*. New Haven: Yale University Press, 1962.

———. *Blackfoot Lodge Tales: The Story of a Prairie People*. Lincoln: University of Nebraska Press, 1971.

———. *The Fighting Cheyennes*. Norman: University of Oklahoma Press, 1983.

Howard, James H. *The Warrior Who Killed Custer: The Personal Narrative of Chief Joseph White Bull*. Lincoln: University of Nebraska Press, 1967.

Linderman, Frank B. *Plenty-Coups: Chief of the Crows*. Lincoln: University of Nebraska Press, 2002.

Nabokov, Peter. *Two Leggings: The Making of a Crow Warrior*. Lincoln: University of Nebraska Press, 1982.

Schultz, James Willard. *Blackfoot and Buffalo: Memories of Life Among the Indians*. Norman: University of Oklahoma Press, 1981.

Smith, Decost. *Red Indian Experiences*. London: George Allen & Unwin Ltd, 1949.

Stands In Timber, John & Liberty, Margot. *Cheyenne Memories*. New Haven: Yale University Press, 1998.